LOTTA
SAYS
'NO!'

Books by Astrid Lindgren

Pippi Longstocking
Pippi Goes Aboard
Pippi in the South Seas

Emil's Clever Pig
Emil and the Great Escape
Emil and the Sneaky Rat

Lotta Says, 'No!'
Lotta Makes a Mess

Karlson Flies Again
Karlson on the Roof
The World's Best Karlson

The Brothers Lionheart

Ronia, the Robber's Daughter

Mio's Kingdom

ASTRID LINDGREN

LOTTA SAYS 'NO!'

Translated by
Tom Geddes

Illustrated by
Tony Ross

OXFORD
UNIVERSITY PRESS

OXFORD
UNIVERSITY PRESS

Great Clarendon Street, Oxford OX2 6DP
Oxford University Press is a department of the University of Oxford.
It furthers the University's objective of excellence in research, scholarship,
and education by publishing worldwide in
Oxford   New York
Auckland   Cape Town   Dar es Salaam   Hong Kong   Karachi
Kuala Lumpur   Madrid   Melbourne   Mexico City   Nairobi
New Delhi   Shanghai   Taipei   Toronto
With offices in
Argentina   Austria   Brazil   Chile   Czech Republic   France   Greece
Guatemala   Hungary   Italy   Japan   Poland   Portugal   Singapore
South Korea   Switzerland   Thailand   Turkey   Ukraine   Vietnam
Oxford is a registered trade mark of Oxford University Press
in the UK and in certain other countries

This translation of *Lotta Says, 'No!'* originally published in Swedish
published by arrangement with Saltkråkan Förvaltning AB

The moral rights of the author, illustrator, and translator have been asserted

First published as *Barnen på Bråkmakargatan* by Rabén & Sjögrn Bokförlag
First published in Great Britain by Methuen & Co Ltd 1968
First published in this edition 2008 by Oxford University Press
First published in this Book People pack 2013

Database right Oxford University Press (maker)

British Library Cataloguing in Publication Data

Data available

ISBN: 978-0-19-273391-7

1 3 5 7 9 10 8 6 4 2

Printed and bound by CPI Group (UK) Ltd, Croydon, CR0 4YY

Paper used in the production of this book is a natural,
recyclable product made from wood grown in sustainable forests.
The manufacturing process conforms to the environmental
regulations of the country of origin.

Contents

Lotta is such a baby

My brother is called Joe and my name is Mary-Lou, and our little sister is called Lotta. Lotta is only just four years old. Daddy says that before there were any children in the house everything was perfectly peaceful. But afterwards there was a constant hullabaloo. My brother was born before me. And Daddy says the house was full of banging and screaming almost straight away, from the moment Joe was big enough to hit his rattle against the side of his cot while Daddy was still trying to sleep on Sunday mornings. And from then on Joe just got

3

noisier and noisier. So Daddy calls him Big Shriek. And he calls me Little Shriek. Though I don't make as much noise as Joe does at all. Sometimes I'm quiet for ages. Then we got another baby, and that was Lotta. Daddy calls her Little Shrill, but I don't know why. Mummy calls us Joe and Mary and Lotta, our real names. Sometimes she calls me Mary-Lou, and so do Joe and Lotta.

We live in a yellow-painted house on a little street called Candlemaker Street.

'Maybe there were candlemakers living in this street once upon a time, but nowadays there are only troublemakers,' Daddy says. 'I think we'll rename it Troublemaker Street.'

Lotta is upset that she isn't as big as Joe and me. We're both allowed to go as far as the market all on our own, but Lotta isn't. Joe and I go to the market on Saturdays and buy sweets from the old ladies there. But we bring sweets home for Lotta too, just as we're told.

One Saturday it was raining so terribly hard that

we nearly couldn't go at all. But we took Daddy's big umbrella and went anyway, and we bought some red sweets. We walked home eating sweets under the umbrella and that was fun. But Lotta wasn't even allowed to go out in the garden because it was raining so terribly hard.

'What's it raining for?' said Lotta.

'So the wheat and potatoes will grow and we'll have something to eat,' said Mummy.

'Why does it rain on the market, then?' asked Joe. 'Is it to make the sweets grow?'

Mummy just laughed.

When we had gone to bed that night, Joe said to me, 'Mary-Lou, when we go to Grandma and Grandad's, let's not plant carrots in the garden—let's plant sweets instead, that'll be much better.'

'Yes, though carrots are better for our teeth,' I said. 'But let's use my green watering can to water them—the sweets, I mean.'

I felt really happy when I remembered my little green watering can that I had out in the country at Grandma and Grandad's. It was kept on a shelf in the cellar. 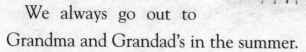 We always go out to Grandma and Grandad's in the summer.

Can you guess what Lotta once did out in the country at Grandma and Grandad's? There's a big dung-heap behind the cowshed, and Mr Johansson takes dung from it and spreads it on the fields to make things grow.

'What's dung for?' asked Lotta. Daddy said that everything grew extra fast if you put dung on it.

'And it has to have rain too,' said Lotta, because she remembered what Mummy had said when it had rained so hard that Saturday.

'Exactly,' said Daddy.

That afternoon it started to rain.

'Has anyone seen Lotta?' Daddy asked.

But we hadn't seen her for a long time, so we went looking for her. First we searched everywhere in the house and in all the wardrobes, but there was no sign of Lotta. Daddy started to get worried, because he had promised Mummy he would look after Lotta. In the end we went to search outside, Joe and Daddy and I, in the cowshed and in the hayloft and everywhere. Then we went behind the cowshed, and—what a surprise—there was Lotta standing in the middle of the dung-heap in all that rain, absolutely sopping wet.

'My poor little Lotta, what are you standing out here for?' said Daddy.

Lotta burst into tears and said, 'So I'll grow and be as big as Joe and Mary-Lou.'

Oh, Lotta is such a baby!

We play all day long

Joe and I play and play and play all day long every day. We let Lotta play with us too when we play the sort of games she can join in. But sometimes we play pirates, and then Lotta just gets in the way. She falls down off the table that we have as our ship. But she screams and wants to join in anyway. When we were playing pirates the other day and Lotta wouldn't leave us in peace, Joe said, 'Do you know what to *do* when you play pirates, Lotta?'

'Stand on the table and jump up and down and be a pirate,' said Lotta.

9

'Yes, but there's a much better way,' said Joe. 'You lie on the floor under the bed absolutely quiet and still . . .'

'What for?' said Lotta.

'Well, you lie there being a pirate, saying very quietly over and over again, "More food, more food, more food",' said Joe. 'That's what pirates do.'

Eventually Lotta came to believe that really was what pirates did, and she crawled under her bed and started saying, 'More food, more food, more food.'

And Joe and I climbed up on the playroom table and sailed away to sea, though it was just pretending, of course.

Lotta lay under her bed all the time saying, 'More food, more food, more food,' and we thought it was almost as much fun watching her as being pirates.

'How long do pirates lie under the bed saying "More food"?' Lotta asked at last.

'Till Christmas,' said Joe.

At that, Lotta crawled out from under the bed

and got up off the floor and said, 'I don't want to be a pirate. They're stupid.'

But sometimes it's good having Lotta with us when we play. Sometimes we play at being angels, Joe and I. We're guardian angels, so we have to have someone to guard, and so we guard Lotta. She has to lie in her bed and we stand beside it swinging our arms and pretending they're wings we're flapping as we fly backwards and forwards. But Lotta doesn't think it's much of a game, because all she has to do is lie still. And when it comes down to it, it's not much different for her from playing pirates, except that then she lies *under* the bed saying 'More food'—otherwise it's the same.

We play doctors and nurses too. Then Joe is a doctor and I'm a nurse and Lotta is a sick child in hospital.

'I don't want to lie in bed,' said Lotta the last time we wanted her to be a sick child. 'I want to be a doctor and put a spoon down Mary-Lou's throat.'

'You can't be a doctor,' said Joe, 'because you can't write persciptions.'

'What can't I write?' said Lotta.

'Persciptions, like the doctor writes, to make sick children better,' said Joe.

Joe can write in capital letters, even though he hasn't started school yet. And he can read too.

At last we got Lotta to lie down on the bed and be ill in hospital, though she really didn't want to.

'So, how are we today then?' said Joe, sounding exactly like the doctor who came to see us when we had measles.

'More food, more food, more food,' said Lotta. 'I'm pretending to be a pirate.'

'Oh, you're silly,' shouted Joe. 'Let's stop, you can't play with us if you're going to be silly.'

And so Lotta let herself be ill in hospital, and we bandaged up her arm, and Joe held a big cotton reel to her chest and could hear through the hole in the middle that she was extremely ill in her chest. And he put a spoon down her throat and could see that she was ill there too.

'I'll have to give her an injection,' he said. Because once when he was ill he was given an injection in the arm by the doctor to make him well again, and that was why he wanted to give Lotta an injection. He went and got a darning needle that we pretended was the kind of needle that doctors have.

But Lotta didn't want an injection. She kicked her legs and screamed, 'You *won't* give me an injection!'

'You idiot, we're only *pretending*,' said Joe. 'Can't you see, I'm not really going to prick you?'

'I don't want an injection anyway,' Lotta yelled.

So we couldn't play doctors and nurses properly any more.

'I'll write out a persciption, anyway,' said Joe. And he sat down at the table and wrote on a piece of paper with a blue crayon. He wrote in capital letters, but I couldn't read it.

Joe and I like playing doctors and nurses. But Lotta doesn't.

SIK GURL MUST BE LOOKED AFTER. SIK GURL HAS TO HAVE INJEXION.
DOCTOR JOE mALM

14

Lotta is as stubborn as a mule

Our dad is so funny. When he comes home from the office we stand in the hall to welcome him, Joe, myself, and Lotta. He laughs and says, 'What a lot of children I've got!'

Once we hid behind the coats in the hall and kept really, really quiet, and then Daddy said to Mummy, 'How come there's no shrieking in the house? Aren't the children well?'

Then we jumped out from behind the coats laughing at him and he said, 'You mustn't frighten me like that. Banging and crashing and shrieking is what I expect when I come home, so it only worries me if there isn't any.'

Well, mostly he doesn't need to worry.

Once two lorries crashed into each other in the street right outside our house, and there was such a terrific noise that Lotta woke up, even though she had only just gone to sleep. And she said, 'What's Joe done now?'

She must think Joe is the cause of all the banging and crashing in the whole world.

Lotta is very sweet and has such chubby legs. Joe and I like kissing Lotta and hugging her, but she doesn't like it. There's lots she doesn't like. She won't take medicine, though she has to when she's ill. Last week she had a cough and Mummy wanted her to take some cough medicine. But Lotta just clenched her teeth and shook her head.

'You're very silly, Lotta,' said Joe.

'I'm not silly,' said Lotta.

'Yes, you are, because you won't take your cough medicine,' said Joe. 'When *I* have to take medicine,

I just *make up my mind* to take it, and then I take it.'

Lotta said, 'When *I* have to take medicine, I just make up my mind *not* to take it, and then I don't take it.'

Then she clenched her teeth again and shook her head from side to side. Mummy patted her and said, 'Well, you'll just have to lie here and cough then, poor little Lotta!'

'Yes, and not sleep a single wink,' said Lotta, rather pleased with herself.

Lotta doesn't like going to bed at night, and nor do I really. I think Mummy is odd, because she wants us to go to bed at night when we feel wide awake, but in the mornings when we're fast asleep, she wants us to get up.

It would have been a good idea for Lotta to take her medicine anyway, because the next day she was coughing and snuffling more than ever, and Mummy said she wasn't to go out. But I had to go to the shop for Mummy, and as I was standing in the queue Lotta came scampering in, all snuffly.

'Go back home,' I said.

'Shan't,' said Lotta. 'I want to come to the shop too.'

Her nose was running like anything, and eventually a lady in the shop said, 'Haven't you got a hanky, little girl?'

'Yes, but I don't lend it to people I don't know,' Lotta replied.

I can tell you even more things about Lotta. Mummy took us to the dentist once, Joe, me, and Lotta. Mummy had seen a little hole in one of Lotta's teeth and she wanted the dentist to mend it.

'If you're a really good girl at the dentist's, I'll give you five kronor,' Mummy said to Lotta.

Mummy had to sit in the waiting room while we were in with the dentist. He looked at my teeth first, but I didn't have any holes, so I was sent back out to Mummy in the waiting room. We sat there for ages waiting for Joe and Lotta, and Mummy said, 'It's amazing that Lotta isn't screaming!'

After some time the door opened and Lotta came out.

'Have you been a brave girl?' said Mummy.

'Yes,' said Lotta.

'What did the dentist do?' Mummy asked.

'He pulled out a tooth,' said Lotta.

'And you didn't scream! Oh, what a brave girl you are,' said Mummy.

'No, I didn't scream.'

'Well, you certainly were a brave girl,' said Mummy. 'Here's a five kronor piece for you.'

Lotta took the five kronor piece and stuffed it in her pocket, looking really pleased.

'Can I see if it's bleeding?' I said.

Lotta opened her mouth, but I couldn't see any missing tooth.

'He didn't take any out,' I said.

'Yes, he did . . . from Joe,' said Lotta.

Then out came Joe, followed by the dentist. The dentist pointed at Lotta and said, 'I couldn't do anything with this little lady, because she wouldn't open her mouth.'

'That baby makes you ashamed of her wherever you go,' said Joe on the way home.

'I didn't know him,' said Lotta. 'I won't open my mouth for people I don't know.'

Daddy says Lotta is as stubborn as a mule.

Mrs Berg is the nicest lady in the world

In the house next door to us lives Mrs Berg, and we go and call on her sometimes. There's a fence between her garden and ours, but we can climb over it, Joe and I. Lotta can't climb it, but Mrs Berg's dog has dug away the earth under the fence in one place, so there's a hole that Lotta can crawl through.

We were at Mrs Berg's the other day and having such fun. She's got a writing-desk that's full of tiny drawers with exciting things in them.

'Please, Mrs Berg, may we look at all your treasures?' asked Joe.

Yes, we could. So first we looked at the doll that Mrs Berg used to play with when she was a little girl. It's called Rosie.

Mrs Berg is old, very old, although not as old as Lotta imagines. What do you think Lotta said?

'Mrs Berg, did you have Rosie with you on Noah's Ark?'

Because just the night before, Daddy had told us the story of Noah's Ark. He told us how Noah built himself a big boat that was called the Ark. And then it poured with rain for weeks on end and everyone who wasn't on Noah's Ark was drowned, and it all happened thousands and thousands of years ago.

Mrs Berg laughed and said, 'Lotta, my pet, I wasn't there on Noah's Ark, you know.'

'Why didn't you drown, then?' said Lotta.

Rosie was in the writing-desk in one of the little drawers she has as her bed. There's pink cotton underneath her and a piece of green satin as a cover, and she herself wears a blue dress. And what's more, in one of the other drawers Mrs Berg has a tiny little basket made of glass with pink roses on. We were allowed to play with Rosie and put the glass basket on her arm, and we pretended she was Little Red Riding Hood taking her grandma some food and drink. Mrs Berg had some chocolates in a bowl on the piano. Some were like small bottles wrapped in silver paper. We put one of the bottles in Little Red Riding Hood's basket with some raisins and almonds that Mrs Berg gave us. And Mrs Berg's dog Scottie was the wolf, and I was Grandma, and Joe was the hunter who comes and shoots the wolf.

'But what about me?' said Lotta. 'Can't I be *anything*?'

We let Lotta carry Rosie and say Little Red Riding Hood's words, because Rosie herself can't talk. But when Little Red Riding Hood got to Grandma's cottage, which was in Mrs Berg's sitting room, there were no raisins left in the glass basket and no almonds either.

'Where's the food for Grandma?' asked Joe.

'Rosie's eaten it,' said Lotta.

So Joe didn't want Lotta playing Little Red Riding Hood with us any more. And Scottie didn't want to join in and pretend to eat up Grandma. Joe held him but he just wriggled and wriggled and wriggled, until in the end he broke free and crept under the sofa and just stuck his nose out from time to time with an angry look at us. Scottie doesn't really like it when we come to Mrs Berg's.

But we had great fun anyway, and we looked at all the other things in Mrs Berg's writing-desk. She's got a pincushion made of red satin in the shape of a heart, and a little picture in a gold frame of a beautiful angel with long blond hair and a white nightdress and two big white wings on its back. Lotta is very fond of that picture, and so am I.

'But how did the angel manage to get the nightie over its wings?' asked Lotta.

Joe said perhaps there was a zip at the back.

Mrs Berg made waffles for us. She does that sometimes when we come to visit her, but not always.

'It's such a lovely summer day that we can sit out in the garden and drink chocolate and eat waffles,' she said.

While Mrs Berg was out in the kitchen making waffles we were left alone to play in the living room. There were two windows in the room and they were open because it was so warm. Joe and I stuck our heads out of the windows, and Joe threw me a marble that he had in his trouser pocket. And I threw it back to him, and so we went on throwing it backwards and forwards. But in the end I dropped it and it fell down on to the lawn. So Joe and I tried to see

who could lean furthest out of the window. We kept
on trying to outdo each other, until all of a sudden
Joe fell right out. I was really frightened. And Mrs
Berg was frightened too. She came into the room
just as Joe fell. She rushed over to the window and
shouted, 'Joe, what's happened?'

Joe was sitting on the lawn with a big bump on
his forehead.

'Mary-Lou and I were seeing who could lean
furthest out of the window, and I won,' he said.

But while Joe and I were trying to outdo one

another, Lotta had discovered Mrs Berg's knitting on the sofa. Mrs Berg knits jumpers and cardigans for people to buy from her. And what do you think? That silly Lotta had pulled out the knitting needles and unravelled all Mrs Berg's knitting! She was sitting on the sofa completely tangled up in wool and tugging and clawing at it.

'Lotta, what have you done?' shrieked Mrs Berg.

'Jumper,' said Lotta. 'The wool has gone all crinkly.'

Then Mrs Berg said it might be best if we went out in the garden and ate our waffles, and that it might be best if we went home after that.

We sat in Mrs Berg's garden and drank chocolate

 and ate lots and lots of waffles with sugar on. It was so lovely in the sun, and there were little sparrows hopping around

us and pecking up crumbs that we threw them. But Mrs Berg soon felt tired and said we had to go home.

So we climbed over the fence, Joe and I, and Lotta crawled through the hole underneath, and we went home and into the kitchen to see what we were going to have for dinner.

'We're having fish in white sauce,' said Mummy.

Joe said, 'It's just as well our tummies are full of waffles, then.'

'I see, so you've been to Mrs Berg's,' Mummy said. 'Was she pleased to see you?'

'Yes,' said Joe. 'She was pleased twice. She was pleased when we came, and she was pleased when we left.'

Mrs Berg is the nicest lady in the world.

We go out for the day

One day Daddy said, 'We're going out for the day on Sunday!'

'Hurrah!' said Joe and I.

'Hurrah, we're going out for the day!' said Lotta.

When Sunday came, Mummy got up early and made pancakes and sandwiches and flasks of hot chocolate for us and coffee for Daddy and herself. We took some lemonade with us too.

When Daddy brought the car round to the door he said, 'Now, let's see whether we can find room for everything in this wretched little car. Let's see whether I can squeeze in Mummy and Big Shriek and Little Shriek and Little Shrill and twenty-six pancakes and I don't know how many sandwiches . . .'

'And Teddy,' said Lotta.

Teddy is a big pink stuffed pig that belongs to Lotta and that she absolutely has to have with her everywhere she goes. She thinks he's a bear and that's why she calls him Teddy.

'But it's definitely a pig and always has been,' says Joe.

That makes Lotta scream, 'No, he's a bear!'

'Bears aren't pink like that,' says Joe. 'Do you think it's a polar bear or an ordinary bear?'

'It's a piggybear,' says Lotta.

Lotta took her piggybear with her for the day. When we were in the car she said, 'Mummy, do pigs have babies?'

'Do you mean Teddy or do you mean real pigs

like the ones out at Grandma and Grandad's?' said Mummy.

Lotta said she meant real live pigs and not bears like Teddy. Mummy said that of course real live pigs had babies.

'No, they don't,' said Joe.

'Of course they do,' said Mummy.

'No, they don't have babies,' said Joe. 'They have *piglets*.'

That made us all laugh, and Daddy said there weren't any children anywhere who were as smart as Big Shriek and Little Shriek and Little Shrill.

We drove out to a small lake and Daddy parked the car on a forest track. We carried all our picnic bags to the edge of the lake. There was a long jetty going out over the water, and Joe and I and Lotta wanted to go out on it and see if we could spot any fish. Mummy lay down on the grass straight away and said to Daddy, 'I'm going to lie here all day long and not move an inch. You can look after the children!'

Daddy came out on the jetty with us and we lay on our tummies and watched all the hundreds of tiny little fish swimming around really fast. Then Daddy made fishing rods for us from long sticks that he cut in the forest, and he tied strings on, with a pin for a hook. We baited them with breadcrumbs on the hooks and sat fishing for ages, but we didn't catch any fish.

After that, we went for a walk in the forest, though Mummy said we mustn't go too far.

We saw a little bird fly into a bush and then fly off again. We went to have a look, and there in the branches of the bush almost down at ground level was a bird's nest with four tiny blue eggs in it.  Oh, they were the prettiest eggs I've ever seen! Lotta wanted to stay there looking at the bird's nest, and she held Teddy up so that he could have a look as well. But Joe and I knew of a good climbing tree nearby and we wanted to go and climb it, so

Lotta had to come with us even though she didn't want to.

I'm very good at climbing trees and so is Joe. But Lotta isn't. We helped her climb up a little way before she started screaming, 'Let me down, let me down!'

And when she was back on the ground she glared really furiously at the tree and said, 'It's crazy to climb trees like that!'

Then Mummy called us to come and eat and we went running back to the lake. She had spread

a plastic tablecloth on the grass and even put cowslips in a glass in the middle and set out all the sandwiches and pancakes and everything.

We sat on the grass to eat. It's much more fun than sitting round a table. The pancakes were really nice, because we had sugar *and* jam on them. The sandwiches were good too. I liked the ones with cold meat in best, and Joe liked the ones with egg and anchovy, so we swapped over. Lotta likes all sandwiches best so she didn't want to swap with anyone. She eats a lot. She had only ever been not hungry once, when she was ill, and Mummy was upset because she wouldn't eat. Then one evening when she was saying her prayers Lotta said, 'Dear Lord, make me want to eat food again. But not fishcakes!'

We were all given our lemonade, Joe and Lotta and myself. Lotta got some sand from the beach to put in hers, and when we asked her why she was doing that she said she just wanted to see what it tasted like.

After we'd eaten Daddy stretched out on the grass and said, 'It's so lovely here in the sun. I think I'll have a nap. You children can look after yourselves for a while. But remember, you're not to go out on the jetty.'

We didn't go out on the jetty. But a little way away there was quite a high flat rock at the edge of the lake and we climbed on to that. Joe said he would show us what Daddy does when he dives in head first.

'This is how he does it,' Joe said, stretching his arms up in the air and doing a little jump. And believe it or not, he tumbled straight into the lake without even meaning to. And to make matters worse, Mummy had told us we weren't to go in the water yet, because it was still much too cold.

Joe sank right under and Lotta and I screamed as loudly as we could. I picked up a branch lying on the ground and when Joe came up again he grabbed hold of it and held on tight. Lotta just started laughing, but Mummy and Daddy came running straight over and Daddy pulled Joe out of the water.

'Joe, whatever do you think you were doing?' said Mummy as Joe stood on the beach completely drenched.

'He was only going to show us what Daddy does,' said Lotta, bursting with laughter at Joe. His trousers looked so funny, she said.

Joe had to take all his clothes off and Mummy hung them up in a tree to dry. But they still weren't dry by the time we were ready to go home, so Joe had to sit in the car wrapped in a blanket. And that made Lotta laugh too. Though all of a sudden she stopped laughing. Because as we were about to drive off, we couldn't find Teddy. We searched high and low, but Teddy had completely disappeared, and Mummy said we would have to go home without him. That made Lotta scream even louder than when Joe fell in the lake.

'Teddy can have a nice night in the forest all on

his own,' said Daddy. 'And I can drive back in the morning and hunt for him.'

But Lotta just went on screaming.

'A goblin might come and scare him,' she said.

'If Teddy met a goblin, I think it would be the goblin who'd be more scared,' said Daddy.

'Can you remember when you had Teddy last?' Mummy asked.

Lotta thought hard.

'Twelve o'clock,' she said.

But Lotta can't tell the time yet, so she'd just made that up. Daddy says Lotta is a shameless child who just says anything that comes into her head.

But I remembered Lotta having Teddy when we were looking at the bird's nest. So we all went back to the tree we'd climbed, because Joe and I knew the nest was somewhere nearby.

And there, by the bush with the bird's nest in, was

Teddy. Lotta picked him up and kissed him on the nose and said, 'Dear Teddy, have you been here all this time looking at those pretty little eggs!'

Joe said the poor mummy-bird probably hadn't dared come back to her eggs all day, because piggy-bears are the best scarecrows in the world, according to him.

That made Lotta angry, and she said, 'Teddy hasn't done any harm. He's just been sitting there looking at the pretty little eggs.'

And so we drove home, with Joe sitting wrapped in his blanket all the way.

Mummy and Daddy came into our bedroom later on to say goodnight to us as they always do. Daddy leant over Lotta's bed where she was lying with a very dirty Teddy beside her.

'Well, my little Lotta,' he said, 'what was the most fun part of the whole day today? I should think it was when we found Teddy, wasn't it?'

'No, the best bit was when Joe fell in the lake,' said Lotta.

We go to Grandma and Grandad's

In the summer we go with Mummy to Grandma and Grandad's in the country. Daddy comes too when he has his holiday. We go by train, because Mummy can't drive the car.

'Now, you mind you're good on the train, so you don't cause too much trouble for Mummy,' Daddy said this summer as he was seeing us off at the station.

'Do we just have to be good on the train?' asked Joe.

'No, everywhere,' said Daddy.

'You *said* it was only on the train we had to be good,' said Lotta.

But the train was already starting to move, so Daddy only managed a wave in reply, and we waved back and shouted goodbye.

We had a compartment almost to ourselves. There was just enough room for one old man to squeeze in. Lotta had brought her Teddy and I had my biggest doll, called Maud Yvonne Marlaine.

The old man had a wart on his chin, and when he went and stood at the window in the corridor for a while, Lotta whispered rather loudly to Mummy, 'That old man's got a wart on his chin . . . '

'Shush,' Mummy whispered, 'he can hear you.'

Lotta looked surprised and said, 'Doesn't he know he's got a wart on his chin?'

Then the guard came to punch our tickets. It was only Mummy and Joe who had tickets, because Lotta and I still travel free.

'How old is this little girl, then?' asked the guard, pointing at me. I said I was nearly six.

He didn't ask how old Lotta was, because he could see she was too small to need a ticket, but Lotta said, 'I'm four and Mummy is thirty-two. And this is Teddy.'

The guard laughed at that and said all Teddys travelled free on this train.

At first we sat still and looked out of the window, but we soon got tired of that. Joe and I went out into the corridor and into other compartments and talked to people we didn't know. We went back to Mummy from time to time so that she didn't get worried. She was telling Lotta stories one after another to keep Lotta sitting still. She didn't want

Lotta going out into the corridor because, as she said, you never knew what Lotta would get up to.

'Tell me the story of Billygoat Gruff, or else I'll go out in the corridor,' said Lotta.

We ate sandwiches and drank lemonade on the train. Then all of a sudden Lotta took a slice of salami out of her sandwich and stuck it on the windowpane. Mummy got very cross with her and said, 'Why have you stuck salami on the window?'

'Because it sticks better than meatballs,' Lotta replied.

That made Mummy even more cross with her. And Mummy had to rub the window with kitchen paper really really hard to clean all Lotta's salami off it.

Once when the train stopped at a station Joe decided that he and I should get off for a little while for some fresh air. We couldn't manage to open the door ourselves, but a lady helped us.

'Are you actually getting off at this station?' she asked.

'Yes,' we said.

Because we *were* getting off, but we would be getting back on again, of course.

When we'd got down from the train we went right along to the end, and just as the train was about to depart we jumped into the last carriage and walked all the way through the train till we came back to our own compartment. As we reached it we saw Mummy and the lady who had helped us with the door standing talking to the guard and Mummy was shouting, 'You *must* stop the train! My children have got off!'

We turned up at that very instant, and Joe said, 'But we got on again.'

Mummy burst into tears, and the guard and the woman who had helped us open the door scolded us. Though why the lady should tell us off when

45

she was the one who had helped us, I really don't know.

'Now go in and sit down in the compartment with Lotta and don't move from the spot,' said Mummy.

But Lotta wasn't in the compartment. She had vanished. Mummy nearly burst into tears again. Off we all went in search of Lotta, and we found her eventually in a compartment a long way down the corridor where she was busy talking to a whole lot of people, and we heard her saying, 'We've got a man in our compartment who's got a wart on his face and doesn't even know it.'

Mummy took hold of Lotta and dragged her away to our own compartment, and there we had to sit perfectly, perfectly still, because Mummy was angry with us and said it would be easier looking after a whole herd of frisky calves than looking after us.

That made me think of the calves I would soon be seeing at Grandma and Grandad's. Which cheered me up no end.

Grandma and Grandad were standing on the verandah to meet us when we arrived. And their dog, whose name was Luke, was barking and leaping up and down, and the garden smelt of summer.

'Are these my little sweethearts arriving?' said Grandma.

'*Your* little sweethearts, maybe,' said Mummy.

'Tomorrow you can have a ride on Chestnut,' said Grandad.

'Come down to the barn with me now, and you can see Pussy's kittens,' said Grandma.

Lotta tugged at Grandma's apron and said, 'Have you still got any sweets in the cupboard, Grandma?'

'Well, I might have,' said Grandma. 'There might be a few little sweets in the cupboard.'

Then I knew we were back at Grandma and Grandad's.

Lotta says a naughty word

There are so many exciting things to do at Grandma and Grandad's. They even have a big tree with a real tree house in it, just like Grandma's verandah. Right up in the tree! There are steps going up to it, and at the top of the steps you climb straight on to the deck of the verandah and there's a table with benches at it and a fence round the whole lot so you don't fall off. Grandma calls it the Leafy Summerhouse. Of all the places there are to sit and eat, I like it best up in trees.

When we woke up on our first morning, Joe

asked straight away, 'Grandma, can we decide now that we'll eat in the Leafy Summerhouse all the time?'

'Oh dear,' said Grandma, 'what do you think Maggie would have to say about it if she had to carry food up those rickety steps three times a day?'

'I'd say not likely!' said Maggie.

Maggie is Grandma's home help. She's very nice, but she doesn't like eating in trees.

'But, Grandma, *we* could carry our food up ourselves,' I said.

'Or else we'll get very cross,' said Lotta. She really is a bit silly, is Lotta!

Grandma said she didn't want Lotta getting cross, so we could take some pancakes with us up into the Leafy Summerhouse.

She cooked loads of pancakes and put them in a basket for us with a bag of sugar and a little jar of jam. She also gave us plates and forks and a bottle of milk and three tin mugs.

So then we climbed up into the Leafy Summerhouse. Joe went up first with the basket, followed by me, followed by Lotta.

'I'd laugh if you dropped the basket, Joe,' said Lotta.

But, Joe didn't drop the basket, and we laid everything out on the table up in the tree and sat on the benches and ate our pancakes with lots of jam and sugar on and drank our milk, with the breeze blowing gently through the leaves. There was such an awful lot of pancakes that Lotta couldn't eat all hers. So what do you think she did? She hung them up in the branches of the tree!

'I'm pretending they're leaves,' she said.

The pancakes were swaying to and fro in the wind and almost did look like leaves.

'Be careful Mummy doesn't catch you,' I said.

But Lotta didn't pay any attention to what I said. She just sat there looking at her pancakes and singing a song that Daddy sings that begins, 'The leaves rustling in the breeze . . . '

She was soon hungry again, and she trotted round taking a bite out of every pancake, so that soon only half-pancakes were left dangling from the branches.

'I'm pretending to be a little lamb grazing on leaves in the woods,' she explained.

Just at that instant a bird came flying by, and Lotta said to it: '*You* can eat my pancakes, but Joe and Mary-Lou can't.'

 But the bird didn't want any pancakes. Though Joe and I felt hungry again, so I held out my hand to Lotta and said, 'Please feed the poor beggarwoman!'

Lotta gave me a pancake she had taken a bite out of, and I put sugar and jam on it and ate it, and it was jolly good, even though it was only half a pancake. And Lotta gave Joe some pancakes too when he said 'Please feed the poor beggar-man!', because Lotta likes anything that's a bit silly. In the end we ate up all Lotta's pancakes, and she said, 'There are no more pancake leaves left. You've got to eat the green ones now!'

And she tore off a whole handful of green leaves and tried to make us eat them. But Joe and I said we were full up.

'They'll be nice with sugar and jam on,' said Lotta, and she spread sugar and jam on a green leaf and ate it herself.

'Watch out for caterpillars on the leaves,' said Joe.

'The caterpillars can watch out for themselves,' said Lotta.

She gets some funny ideas in her head, does Lotta, Grandad says. The next day, which was a Sunday, we had fish for dinner, the worst thing Lotta can think of (except for fishcakes). The weather was beautiful, and whenever it's like that, Grandma and Grandad always eat out in the garden, at a table under the biggest tree. We were all sitting round the table, Grandma and Grandad and Mummy and Joe and me, but Lotta was still playing with the cat and wouldn't come even when Mummy kept on calling her. When she finally appeared and saw we were eating fish, she said, 'Oh, hell, not fish on Sunday!'

That made Mummy very cross with her, because she's told Lotta a hundred times she mustn't say 'hell', which is really a naughty word. Mummy said

that if Lotta said 'hell' once more, she wouldn't be allowed to stay with Grandma and Grandad a day longer, but would have to go back to town. And she wasn't allowed to sit with us and eat because she had said that, and she went round the garden screaming all the time we were eating.

She was told to sit at the table and eat by herself afterwards, but she just went on screaming. Mummy sent Joe and me away to play so that Lotta was left on her own till she was good again. But we stood watching her round the corner as she went on screaming and screaming. When she finally quietened down, it was only because she had got another one of her strange ideas in her head. She picked up the fish from her plate and went over to the rainwater tub under the roof-gutter, and dropped the fish in it. Mummy came by right at that moment and heard Lotta say, 'It can go to hell and swim for a bit!'

'Lotta, do you remember what I told you?'

Lotta nodded, and went off into the house, reappearing a few minutes later carrying her own little suitcase, with a belt hanging out of it dragging on the ground after her as she walked along. And Mummy and Grandma and Grandad and Joe and I all stood and watched her set off. She went up to Grandma and Grandad and gave a little curtsy and said, 'I'm going home to Daddy, because he's much nicer than Mummy.'

She didn't say goodbye to Mummy, nor to Joe and me either. We stood watching her go with the belt trailing behind her. But when she got to the gate she came to a halt. She stood there for some time quite still. Mummy went after her and said, 'Well, little Lotta, aren't you going?'

To which Lotta replied, 'Oh, hell, Mummy, I can't travel on the train all by myself!'

Mummy picked Lotta up and said it might be best if she stayed where she was, because we would all of us be so sad if she went away. And Lotta threw her arms round Mummy's neck and cried and wouldn't speak to Joe and me, though we wanted to make a fuss of her and kiss her.

That night when we were in bed Grandma sat in our bedroom and told us Bible stories and showed us pictures from a beautiful Bible she has. She read us the story of Jonah and the whale, and when Jonah cried out from the belly of hell, Lotta said, 'Oh, Grandma, what was that you said?'

But Lotta herself hardly ever says hell any more.

Lotta's unlucky day

One of the best things of all at Grandma and Grandad's is the play-house that Mummy and Auntie Kate had when they were young. It's red and stands in a corner of the garden with a narrow little path leading up to it and a lawn in front with daisies growing in it. And there's small white furniture inside the play-house, tables and chairs and a cupboard, and in the cupboard is a doll's tea service and a tiny frying pan and a doll's iron and a little jug with glasses to drink out of. Mummy's and Auntie Kate's dolls still live in it. And there's a stool that

Grandma had when *she* was a child—it's hard to imagine a stool could be so old!

One day when we were at Grandma and Grandad's we went to play in the play-house, pretending that Joe was Daddy and I was Mummy and Lotta was the home help, called Maggie.

'Daddy's taking the baby out now,' said Joe straight away, pushing the doll's pram with Auntie Kate's baby doll in it out into the garden.

'And I'm going to scrub the kitchen floor,' said Lotta.

'No, first of all we're going to make some cheese,' I said, because I was the one in charge, since I was Mummy.

'You're not to make any cheese till I've finished scrubbing,' said Lotta.

But Joe and I said Lotta couldn't play if she didn't do as she was told. So we made cheese. To make cheese you put redcurrants and raspberries in a handkerchief and squeeze out all the juice, and what's left in the hanky you make into little round cheeses that are really really sour.

'*Now* can I scrub the kitchen?' asked Lotta.

She picked up the bucket and went off to Grandma's kitchen for water, and then poured nearly all of it over the floor of the play-house and started scrubbing away with a brush she'd already soaped. She was soon wet all over.

'Are you swimming or what?' said Joe, who had come in from taking the baby out in the garden.

'I'm scrubbing the kitchen floor,' Lotta replied.

'The kitchen *has* to be scrubbed, and anyway it's good fun.'

But in the end Joe and I had to help her mop up the water. Lotta didn't want to. She just stood to one side watching us.

Maggie, the *real* Maggie, sings and dances, kicking her legs up and singing 'Tra-la-lah, dumdy-doo, I can see all of you.'

Now Lotta started doing what Maggie does, kicking her legs in the air, but singing, 'Tra-la-lah, dumdy-doo, I'll splash water over you.' And as she said 'splash', she took the whisk that was hanging on the wall of the play-house and dipped it in the bucket and splashed water all over Joe and me, laughing as loudly as she could. That made us so angry that we said if she was as silly as that she could mop up the water herself. But she just went on kicking her legs up and singing, 'I'll splash water over you.' The floor was very slippery from all the soap, and when Lotta kicked her legs up as high as she could, down she fell and hit her head on the cupboard.

Poor old Lotta! That made her scream and cry out, 'It's no fun being Maggie!'

So she went off to find the cat instead, and Joe and I played on our own and made spinach out of lilac leaves and ate cheese and spinach, though only pretend.

Suddenly we heard Lotta screaming outside, and when we looked out we saw her pulling the cat along by its tail, which made the cat so angry that it scratched her. She came running in to us in the play-house and said, 'I was only holding him by his stalk and he scratched me!'

Mummy and Grandma weren't at home, so we went in search of Maggie to get a plaster put on Lotta. Maggie wasn't in the kitchen. But what do you think Lotta had done? She'd forgotten to turn off the tap when she fetched the bucket of water, and all I can say is that there was ten times as much water on the kitchen floor as there was in the play-house when Lotta was scrubbing. Joe waded through all the water and turned off the tap, just as Maggie came in.

She threw up her hands in horror and cried, 'Joe, whatever are you doing?'

'He's swimming,' said Lotta, laughing as loudly as anything. But Maggie wanted to know who had left the tap on, so Lotta admitted, 'I did.'

'Why did you do it?' Maggie asked.

'Because it's not my ducky day.'

Lotta says 'not my ducky day' when she means 'not my lucky day', one when everything goes wrong. I think it's not Lotta's lucky day nearly all the time.

But Maggie mopped the floor and put a plaster on Lotta and gave us hot chocolate and cakes at the kitchen table and danced for us and sang, 'Tra-la-lah, dumdy-doo, I can see all of you.'

Lotta ate five cakes and Joe ate four and I ate three.

'This is a really fun not ducky day,' said Lotta afterwards. And she hugged Maggie as tightly as she could and sang, 'Tra-la-lah, dumdy-doo, here I am, kissing you.'

And so she was, and Maggie said she was a very special little girl.

Lotta is a slave in prison

Joe and Lotta and I have two cousins who are the children of Auntie Kate. When we were at Grandma and Grandad's in the country in the summer, Auntie Kate was there too and had Anna and Tommy with her. Anna and Tommy are our cousins. Anna is the same age as Joe, and Tommy is a new baby like Lotta. Anna can get the better of Joe in a fight, because she's very strong and very determined. And Lotta can easily get the better of Tommy, and she often does, too, even though Mummy says she mustn't.

'Why do you hit Tommy when he's so nice?' Mummy asked Lotta.

'Because he's so sweet when he cries,' said Lotta.

So Lotta had to sit on her own in the play-house until she was good again. And Anna came up with the idea that we should pretend Lotta was in prison and come to her rescue.

'We'll have to smuggle in some food to her first,' Anna said. 'You only get bread and water in prison.'

So we went into the kitchen and asked Maggie for some meatballs. Anna put them in the little basket that we use for picking berries. Then Joe and Anna climbed up on the roof of the play-house and called to Lotta to say we would lower some food to her down the chimney. But Lotta put her head out of the window and asked why she couldn't have the food through the window or through the door.

'Isn't the door locked?' asked Anna.

'No, it's a really useless prison,' said Lotta. 'Bring the food to me here!'

But that made Anna cross with Lotta and she said

that when you're in prison you had to have food lowered down the chimney to you. 'So there,' she said.

'Go on, then,' said Lotta.

Anna tied a long piece of string to the basket and lowered it down the chimney. She let Joe help a bit, though not much. But Tommy and I just had to stand below and watch.

'Here it comes!' yelled Lotta inside the play-house. 'And lots of soot, too,' she added. Tommy and I peered through the window and saw Lotta eating the food.

But it was covered in soot and Lotta's hands and face were turning very black. Anna said that was good, because now Lotta could be a captured slave that we could free. So Lotta smeared even more soot on herself to make herself look like a real slave. But Tommy cried because he thought slaves were dangerous.

'Of course they're not dangerous,' said Anna.

'But they look dangerous,' said Tommy, crying even more.

This pleased Lotta and she pulled faces at Tommy and said, '*Some* slaves are quite dangerous.'

Then she went on, 'Free me now! I want to go round scaring people. I like people being scared of me.'

Anna and Joe decided we should free Lotta through the window at the back. We went and got the seesaw, because Anna said it could be a bridge across the ditch round the prison. We put the seesaw against the window, and Anna and Joe and I all climbed in to free the slave. All of us except Tommy. He just stood looking on and crying.

When we got into the play-house, Lotta wasn't there. Anna was angry.

'Where's that baby got to now?' she shouted.

'I've escaped,' said Lotta when we found her. She was sitting under the redcurrant bushes eating currants.

'We were going to free you,' said Anna.

'I freed myself,' said Lotta.

'You're impossible to play with,' said Joe.

'Ha ha,' said Lotta.

Then Mummy came and saw that Lotta wasn't in

the play-house any more. 'Are you going to be good now?' she asked.

'Yes . . . Though I'm a bit black,' said Lotta.

Mummy must have been afraid of slaves too, because she threw up her hands and said, 'My goodness me, what do you look like!'

And Lotta had to go out to the laundry-room and wash herself for a good half hour.

In the afternoon we took the meat basket with us and went out to pick wild strawberries. There are so many wild strawberries in the meadows at Grandma and Grandad's. But, oh dear, we were scared when we were picking them, because we saw a snake. The only one who wasn't scared was Tommy.

'Look, there's a tail without a bow-wow,' he said. He didn't know it was a snake.

When we got home Anna divided up all the strawberries so that we had exactly the same number each. Though Anna got the biggest and reddest. Tommy and Lotta sat on the verandah to eat theirs. Then we heard Tommy crying. Auntie Kate put her head out of the window and asked, 'Why's Tommy crying?'

'He's crying because I won't let him have any of my strawberries,' said Lotta.

'Have his own strawberries all gone?' Auntie Kate asked.

'Yes,' said Lotta, 'they've all gone. And he cried when I ate them too.'

Then out came Mummy and took away Lotta's strawberries and gave them to Tommy, and Lotta said, 'Tra-la-lah, off to bed I go.'

'I think you'd better,' said Mummy. 'You must be tired by now, Lotta.'

'Oh, no, I'm not,' said Lotta. 'My legs still feel bouncy. But I'll go to bed anyway.'

However, that night Lotta was really nice to Tommy. Tommy was supposed to sleep in the little guest room all on his own. But he was afraid of the dark and cried and wanted the door left open.

Auntie Kate said, 'But, Tommy, you're never afraid of sleeping in the dark at home.'

Lotta said, 'That's different, Auntie Kate, that's his own dark at home. He's not used to Grandma's dark, it's different.'

So Tommy was allowed to sleep in the same room as me and Joe and Lotta. And Lotta kissed him and tucked him in and said, 'I'll sing to you and then you won't be afraid.'

And then she sang the same lullaby as Mummy sings to us:

> Till the night is over
> May Thine angels spread
> Their white wings above you
> Watching round your bed.

'And Lotta's too,' said Lotta. 'And I'm not a slave!'

We have such fun at Christmas

One day Joe asked me, 'Which do you like best, the sun or the moon or the stars?'

I said I liked them all the same. But maybe the stars just a tiny bit more, because they twinkle so prettily when we go to church at Christmas. And I like Christmas a lot too.

This Christmas, I wanted a pair of skis. So I was really afraid there wouldn't be any snow. Lotta wanted it to snow too, because she was hoping for a sledge.

After we were in bed one night not long before

Christmas, Lotta said, 'I've asked Daddy for a sledge, so now I have to ask God for snow, or I won't be able to go sledging.'

So this is what she said: 'Dear God, please make it snow now, straight away. Think of all the poor flowers that need a warm blanket while they're asleep under the ground and feeling so cold.'

Then she peeked over the side of the bed and said to me, 'I was clever this time, I didn't say I wanted the snow for my sledge.'

And believe it or not, when we woke up the next day it had started snowing! Joe and Lotta and I stood at the window in our pyjamas and watched more and more snowflakes falling outside, in our garden and in Mrs Berg's. We got dressed as fast as we could and ran outside to throw snowballs, and we made a jolly good snowman that Daddy put his hat on when he came home.

We really enjoyed ourselves all day long, and Mummy was pleased we were outside because Mrs Hill had come to help her make the house nice for

Christmas. Lotta likes talking to Mrs Hill and calls her by her first name, even though Mummy says she shouldn't. Lotta should call her 'Mrs Hill', Mummy says. Mrs Hill likes talking to Lotta, but Mummy says she shouldn't answer if Lotta doesn't call her Mrs Hill properly.

The day we made the snowman, when we were back indoors eating our breakfast, Lotta said to Mrs Hill, 'Hey, feel how wet my gloves are!'

When Mrs Hill didn't answer, Lotta said, 'Have you seen our snowman?'

But Mrs Hill still didn't answer. Lotta was silent for a long time, and then she said, 'Hell, what are you so cross about, Mrs Hill?'

Mummy said, 'Lotta, you know that you mustn't say "hell" and that you must use Mrs Hill's name properly.'

'Well, I don't think I can talk to her at all, then,' said Lotta.

Mrs Hill said the last thing she wanted was Lotta not to talk to her, so she asked Mummy if Lotta could call her by her first name. At which Mummy laughed and agreed that Lotta could.

'And say "hell" too?' Lotta asked.

'No, not "hell",' said Mummy.

When Mummy had gone out, Lotta said, 'I know what I'll do. When I mean "hell" I'll say "Hill". Because Mummy likes me saying "Hill".'

Then she said, 'Oh, Hill, what fun it is at Christmas.'

And it really is—fun, I mean. Joe and Lotta and I helped Mummy with all the Christmas preparations

and shovelling snow off
the path and putting out a
Christmas table for the
birds. Mummy thought we
worked very hard.

'I don't know what I'd do if I didn't have you all,'
she said.

Lotta dried the knives and forks very carefully
every day, and she said, 'I don't know what I'd do if
I didn't have me. But, Hill, it's really hard work!'

We had great fun buying presents too. We took
the money out of our piggy-banks that we'd been
saving all year, and the three of us went into town
to buy presents. It's fun buying presents when
there's snow on the ground and piles of Christmas
trees in the market and masses of people going in
and out of the shops. Joe and I wanted to buy a little
rubber doll for Lotta, so we told her to stay outside
on the street and wait while we went into the toy
shop.

'You mustn't look,' said Joe.

'You can look in the window of the tea-shop instead,' I said.

Lotta was very happy to do that, because there were so many marzipan animals and other goodies in their window.

When Joe and I had bought the rubber doll and come back out on to the street, Lotta had disappeared. But then we saw her coming out of the tea-shop.

'What have you been doing?' asked Joe.

'Buying a Christmas present for you,' Lotta replied.

'What have you bought, then?' said Joe.

'A cream cake,' said Lotta.

'Oh, you idiot, it won't keep till Christmas,' said Joe.

'No, that's what I thought,' said Lotta. 'So I ate it.'

And guess what, at that very moment Daddy came walking along the street. He didn't know we were out on our own buying Christmas presents.

'I have a feeling I've seen these children somewhere before, but I can't remember where,' he said.

'Still, they look very cute, so I think I'll take them to the tea-shop.'

Oh, how delighted we were! We could drink as much chocolate and eat as many cakes as we wanted, and we sat on the big green sofa, and there was a hubbub of conversation all around us, and everyone had Christmas packages that they'd been buying, and it was snowing outside on the street and the cakes and pastries were absolutely *full* of cream—what a lovely day it was. A lady called Mrs Freeman came over to us and started talking to Daddy. Joe and I sat quietly, but Lotta talked more than Mrs Freeman. Until Daddy said, 'Lotta, you mustn't speak when grownups are talking, you should wait till they've finished.'

'Huh,' said Lotta, 'I've tried that, but it doesn't work. They never stop.'

That made Mrs Freeman laugh and she said she must go home and bake some gingerbread men for Christmas.

We baked gingerbread men too, but not till the next day. We made so many that Joe and Lotta

and I all filled our tins, and we made them all
by ourselves. We put the
tins in the playroom, and
we said we would save
the gingerbread men for
Christmas Eve. But Lotta
ate all hers the very same
day and then couldn't eat
her mashed vegetables for dinner in the evening.

'They might not have kept till Christmas,' she
said.

But then she came begging for gingerbread men
from Joe and me every day, saying, 'Please feed the
poor beggar-woman!'

At last Christmas Eve arrived, and it's the most
exciting day of the whole year. I'll tell you what we
did on Christmas Eve.

As soon as we woke up we ran down to the
kitchen, and there was Mummy making coffee.
We all sat down in front of the fire in the living
room drinking coffee, though we children never

get coffee normally. And we had saffron buns and gingerbread men and doughnut-rings with it. The Christmas tree was already standing there and smelt fantastically good. As soon as we'd finished our coffee we decorated the tree, Daddy and Joe and myself and Lotta. Mummy was in the kitchen making salad with spiced herring.

'It's so pretty in our house,' said Joe, 'that I think it's the finest house in the whole town.'

'And the best-smelling,' Lotta added.

Mummy had planted lots of bowls of white

hyacinths that gave out a wonderful smell, and there were candles everywhere and everything looked so different from the way it usually did, and it smelt different too. I like it smelling different at Christmas time.

We ate lots of food all day long, and we ate in the kitchen and dunked bread in the Christmas hambroth on the stove. And in the afternoon we went with Mummy to Mrs Berg's to give her her Christmas presents, and we were given butterscotch and toasted almonds. And Lotta got a nice red hat that Mrs Berg had knitted for her.

'I could almost be Father Christmas now,' said Lotta.

But she couldn't. Because in the evening the real Father Christmas came. He stamped in the porch and thumped on the door and came in with a sack on his back chock-full of Christmas presents.

'I don't need to ask if there are any good children here,' he said, 'because I can see it on your faces.'

And then he added to Lotta, 'Mind your eyes don't pop out of your head!'

Because Lotta was standing there staring at him wide-eyed.

Then Father Christmas went out again and came back in with a big package that had my skis in and a big package with Lotta's sledge in. But Lotta just stood there in silence and didn't move until Father Christmas had gone.

'Why are you so quiet, Lotta?' Mummy asked.

'My tummy tickles when I see Father Christmas,' Lotta replied. 'Oh, Hill, I get such a tickle in my tummy!'

On Christmas Eve we were allowed to stay up as long as we wanted. We sat eating nuts and oranges in front of the fire and we danced round the Christmas tree and everything was so beautiful. And the next day, Christmas Day, we went to church. The bird table outside was covered in snow, but we brushed off the snow so that the sparrows would be able to eat, and then we went to the early morning Christmas service. The stars were still twinkling, and that's why I like the stars best, though the sun and the moon are nice too. When the stars shine on Troublemaker Street, the whole road looks so mysterious. There were lights in nearly all the houses, which made them look very pretty, but mysterious too. Far, far away, right above the roof of the town hall, was a star which was the biggest star I've ever seen.

'That must be the Christmas Star,' said Lotta.

ASTRID LINDGREN

Astrid Lindgren was born in Vimmerby, Sweden in 1907. In the course of her life she wrote over 40 books for children, and has sold over 145 million copies worldwide. She once commented, 'I write to amuse the child within me, and can only hope that other children may have some fun that way too.'

Many of Astrid Lindgren's stories are based upon her memories of childhood and they are filled with lively and unconventional characters. Perhaps the best known is *Pippi Longstocking*, first published in Sweden in 1945. It was an immediate success, and was published in England in 1954.

Awards for Astrid Lindgren's writing include the prestigious Hans Christian Andersen Award and the International Book Award. In 1989 a theme park dedicated to her—Astrid Lindgren Värld—was opened in Vimmerby. She died in 2002 at the age of 94.

Lotta's mischief continues in

LOTTA MAKES A MESS!

Lotta's in a very bad mood! In fact, she's so cross with her own family, she's moved in next door.

But how long will she stay? Because she soon realizes that, sometimes, the best fun is to be had at home...